Bigfoot Sasquatch Files

Volume 7

A Special Christmas Edition

By Kevin E. Lake

These stories are true.

Potentially...

Customer Service Is Dead

(Originally Titled: The Unfortunate Demise Of Karen The Clerk)

Her name wasn't really Karen, but we'll call her that, because she sure as hell acted like a Karen. We must point out, however, that though she was white, she hadn't come from privilege. Just the opposite, actually. Opposite as in you might refer to her as poor white trash and be pretty spot on.

She wasn't bad looking for a woman nearing fifty. However, she wasn't nearing fifty. She was only thirty five. You see, just like everyone whose hearts have been hardened early in life by bitternous, jealousy, rage, and hatred (mostly self-hatred) Karen's outer shell had aged prematurely, letting anyone with a keen eye see just how toxic and venomous she truly was on the inside.

But if you couldn't see these things about Karen with your eyes, and you wanted to find out about them the hard way, all you had to do was go to the post office.

Karen's post office.

Karen had started out as a mail carrier shortly after dropping out of high school. Oh, how she'd hated having to go back and get her G.E.D. in order to get the job, but after Mommy and her Mommy's boyfriend, who had also been Karen's boyfriend (but Mommy never knew, and Karen had been eighteen the first time she and Jim Bob had gotten together, so it *was* legal eagle) died of an overdose together on Christmas Eve of all days, Karen had no choice. If only she'd been a minor when Mommy had passed on, she thought, she could have gotten social security checks for a while- until she could have lassoed some older schmuck of a guy who got them full time because he'd already suckered the SSI Disability people into believing he had a cause worthy of a tax free check for life- but no. Mommy had to go and kill herself with the pills when Karen was already the ripe old age of nineteen, forcing Karen to make an honest effort to enter the workforce and support herself.

No worries, Karen thought, at first. She'd just get herself a somewhat decent paying job and then fake an injury while on said job, then get her one of those SSI disability checks for life, just like the generations of poor white trash that came before her, and hell, it would all work out better in the end, because then she wouldn't need one of those schmucks of a man who was already getting a check, because she'd have her own. As Karen saw it, it was the perfect plan!

Wrong!

These had been the days of the great recession, and Karen found that jobs were few and far between. There was but one hope, as Karen saw it.

Government!

And why not the post office?

Karen sure as shit wasn't going to join the military. Sure, the Army and all the other branches of brave, honorable men and women who fought for the protection of the free world (and the occasional deposit of oil) was always hiring, but Karen was neither brave *nor* honorable. She was lazy, entitled (hey, at least she possessed *that* real Karen traight), and the farthest thing from honorable. Karen cared only about herself, her own basic needs being met, and fuck everyone else, in Karen's mind. The military would not do, but the post office was the perfect fit for her. It was right up her alley. So many people who possessed her shitty attitude and complete lack of concern for quality of work found lifelong careers at the post office. Sure, there were those who worked at the post office who were some of the hardest workers in society, *many* actually- and many with very *positive* attitudes- but at the post office, these folks were the minority. These people made up the ten percent of the post office's work force that carried the other ninety percent for thirty years and to their pensions.

But again, Karen had no desire to spend thirty years at the post office, or at *any* job. She only wanted to work long enough to fake an injury and get herself one of those SSI disability checks for life. Hell, she thought, if she was lucky, she could make it look *really* good and she might even end up getting herself a lifelong prescription for something like Vicodin or Oxycodone and then she wouldn't have to spend any of her hard earned monthly SSI disability check money on pills. Boy, Karen thought, if Mommy were still alive, she'd be so proud!

Long story short (I know, too late) Karen jumped through the necessary hoops to get her G.E.D., she took and passed (with flying colors) the postal exam, and in pretty quick order she found herself shucking mail into the boxes of the shitty little houses in her shitty little Appalachiastanian community for almost twenty dollars an hour, and the pay, she was surprised, was so good, for a minute (well, maybe for half a minute), she actually considered doing the right thing- keeping the job long term, not faking an injury to get her Government money- but alas, she came to her senses, and on a cold, snowy day in February, during the middle of the fourth week of her job as a letter carrier, Karen threw herself down a flight of steps (okay, there were only three steps leading up to a porch, but technically, it counts as a flight), and she landed flat on her back and she began moaning and screaming in agony. Her fall really had hurt, but she wasn't in as much pain as she was letting on to be in, but it was all part of her great plot. In her heart of hearts, with each agonizing scream, that wasn't really that agonizing, Karen knew her lifelong SSI disability check was as good as in the mail!

Wrong!

What Karen had been completely unaware of at the time of her 'fall' was the fact that one of her supervisors had been trailing her, secretly, observing her work. The supervisor, a lifer as they're known in all Government job circles- someone who possesses *no* work ethic, a *shitty* attitude, yet cannot be gotten rid of due to a strong union, and who *always* gets bumped up into management at Government jobs- had actually felt intimidated by Karen up until this point. Despite Karen's shitty attitude, the supervisor knew she was getting her work done in the projected time to do it, and he'd thrown her on some of the longer routes to test her. Actually, to set her up for failure. Little did he know that Karen's shitty attitude was worse than his, and anger and frustration fueled Karen. Though she hated the longer routes, it was the energy derived from that hatred that allowed her to finish them under time.

Ah, the supervisor thought now, watching Karen make snow angels on the walkway of the property where she'd fallen, waiting on the homeowner (or renter, or squatter) to come to her aid, be her witness, and to later be forced by the SSI disability people to write a sworn statement on her behalf so she could get her check. However, the homeowner never came. Unbeknownst to Karen, they'd gone on a Schlitz Malt Liquor run just before she'd reached their house, and the only face that Karen soon saw standing over her, bearing witness to the events that had just taken place, was the face of her supervisor.

"What the fuck, Karen?" he said. "What in the actual fuck?"

"Shit," Karen said from her position on her back on the ground. She knew the jig was up, so she said it again. "Shit!'

***

Karen was summarily fired from the post office for what they perceived as being an attempt to intentionally get injured on the job for the sake of getting an SSI disability check for life. Hey, it was the post office. They were used to it. However, her union, the National Association of Letter Carriers, quickly went to bat for Karen, as they did all the shitbags at the post office (and it is important to note this, for the union rarely represents hard, honest workers who are actually getting screwed by management), and sure enough, Karen got her job back, as well as back pay for the six weeks she'd been out due to having been fired. However, Karen was no longer a mail carrier. Karen was now a clerk.

There were no available clerk spaces where Karen lived, and it had been the post office's hopes that upon having to transfer in order to regain employment with the postal system, that Karen would merely quit and the postal service could wash their hands of her. But no. Not *this* Karen. This Karen was determined to get her SSI disability check for life at all costs, and if she had to actually work for a year or two to let bygones be bygones, then so be it. And just as soon as all those bys were gone, she'd figure out a way to fake an injury in the mailroom, and by God, that SSI check for life would be hers!

Wrong!

They'd not just transferred Karen out of her small town in Appalachiastan, they'd transferred Karen out of Appalachiastan entirely! They'd moved her over the mountain, into Virginia! And not just *any* part of Virginia. They'd moved her to the outskirts of Charlottesville, a town affluent with blue blood trust babies and Virginia first families, both groups of which came from generational wealth, generational ivy league educations, and generational pretentiousness. Karen was now, truly, a fish out of water, surrounded by real Karens and the beta-males they marry.

The postal service was wise enough, at least, not to throw Karen directly into the center of C'ville, as the town was known by locals (as well as Hoo'ville, and not because of Doctor Seuss and that *other* Christmas book- that story of Seuss living in C'ville during the time he wrote *that* book about some grinchy old green bastard and basing it off of the town and town's people and yada yada is all a lie), fearing she'd be so lost in the weeds due to the extremely high volume of mail and packages it received (more in a day than her shithole little town back in Appalachian received in a month) so they put her in one of the tiny little branch offices on the outskirts of town. One of those tiny little post offices that actually closed and locked their doors for an hour for lunch, because there was only one clerk in the branch.

When the postmaster at Karen's previous post had told her that she would be transferring a state away as a condition of keeping her job, and Karen had agreed to the transfer, the post office intentionally chose a spot to put her where she would feel so out of place that she would quit (since the idea of a transfer in and of itself hadn't been enough to do the trick), and the tiny little branch they stuck her in was the perfect spot. You see, volume would not be an issue. The clientele, many of the clientele, at least, would be the ingredient needed to make for the perfect mix of getting almost *anyone* to want to quit the job. To describe them? In a word? Or a few, at least?

Stuck up, pretentious, narcissistic snobs who looked down on anyone who was just not *as* wealthy as them, but who'd not been *born* into wealth like them, meaning, they actually looked down their noses at self made millionaires and even self made billionaires. You see, the affluent of Charlottesville viewed themselves as God's chosen people. Why else, they figured, had they been *born* into affluence, while the other ninety seven percent of the human race had not been? Oh, there was *no way* Karen would feel comfortable in their presence, and she would quit her job in short order, for sure! This, at least, is what the post office's H.R. people had thought.

Wrong!

The post office did not know Karen as well as they thought they did!

***

"Maybe if you'd pull that silver spoon out of your ass, you'd be able to make it down here in time before I close up for lunch," Karen screamed at a middle aged trust baby at 11:59 a.m. on the first day of her second week on the job at her new location. She'd spent her first week with a trainer, but she knew the ropes of the small branch now (there were only two hundred and fifty customers who rented boxes, less than her post office back in Appalachiastan), and Karen had no problem running the show on her own. Oh, and how she *loved* the concept of closing for an hour for lunch.

Nap time!

"It's a birthday card for my mother," the middle aged trust baby said to Karen. "I'm already late in getting it out. I fear if it gets there *too* late, she won't send me my next dividend check. "You know," the woman said, tilting her chin in and her nose up, raising the index finger of her right hand to her pursed lips, "my great grandfather invented velcro. Our family still owns the patent."

"Yeah?" Karen said, coming across as if she gave a shit. The middle aged trust baby, the *real* Karen, bought it for a second, but then not real Karen said, "my great grandfather invented the ass whoopin', and my family still hands them out! Now you go on and get the fuck on outt'a here and come back in an hour, or I'mma whoop your highflutin' ass!"

"Why, I never!" the woman said and then turned to walk out.

"I bet you never, you bitch!" not real Karen the clerk yelled after her. "Can't get them tight ass legs holding that silver spoon up your ass apart long enough to do it!"

Real Karen left and she mailed her mother's birthday card from the main office in C'ville. It got there just before her mother was about to rip up her daughter's dividend check. Real Karen never went back to see fake Karen again.

***

"How much to send this to Philippines?"

Karen heard the voice, but she hadn't seen who it belonged to. She was putting mail in boxes. She looked over at the counter and all she saw was the top of a head. Long, jet black hair.

"What?" Karen said, moving over to the counter. It was only two weeks from Christmas, and ordinarily, every post office in America would be packed with customers, but Karen had been at her post for nine months now. She'd summarily ran off all the regular customers. Those she could not piss off or offend enough into never coming back, she banned. When they'd called the main branch's postmaster to complain, and the postmaster had tried to unban them, Karen's new union, The American Postal Workers Union, jumped in on her behalf, stating that if the area's postmaster were to allow barred customers to return, that they would be putting Karen in an unsafe work environment. As was always the case, the postmaster did not listen to the union, and each time one of Karen's barred customers entered her branch, Karen was awarded five thousand dollars in grievance pay. And though Karen's grievance pay, combined with her salary, was closing in on making it possible for her to actually buy a house in the new highfalutin area she lived and worked in (she was currently renting 'urban' living space in the middle of city limits), she still fully intended on only working another six months or so before faking her injury, this time, she was certain, without witnesses, and finally obtaining that SSI disability check for life.

"How much to send this to Philippines?" the stunningly beautiful, petite Asian woman on the other side of the counter asked. Ironically, this woman, a Filipina beauty who was married to local Cryptozoologist, Dr. (honorary) Drake and Karen were the exact same age. But whereas Karen appeared to be nearing fifty, due to her hardened heart, shitty attitude, and all the other negative attributes of which we're all now fully aware, Mrs. Drake looked like a teenager. She didn't appear to be a day over twenty. Sure, her petite stature and beautiful, Asian complexion helped add to her youthful appearance, but it was the true, beautiful and kind nature of her heart that helped her stay young.

Karen looked down at her watch. It was eleven thirty. Damn it, she thought. She couldn't blow this little oriental bitch off with the closing for lunch excuse. She really wanted to get all the mail put away before lunch so she wouldn't have to deal with it later, and there was something about this little Asian woman she didn't like. There was always something about people who were happy and not toxic that Karen didn't like. Mostly the facts that they were happy and not toxic.

"Cut off for international is at eleven thirty," Karen said, thinking quickly on her feet. "Come back when I reopen at one o'clock."

"No time," Mrs. Drake said. "Many errand."

"Many errand," Karen said, mocking her. "Many errand."

"Why you make me fun?" Mrs Drake asked, feeling a bit of anger beginning to boil up inside her. Sure, Mrs. Drake was a cute little beauty- a true pearl of the orient- but as Mr. Drake could and *would* tell anyone, if you pissed her off, hide the mother fucking machette!

Karen reached up with both hands and grabbed at the outer edges of both of her eyes with her fingers. She pulled her skin tight, making her eyes slant. "Why you make me fun?" she said. "Why you make me fun?"

"Pesti mata, ka!" Mrs. Drake said.

Though Karen did not speak VIsayan, Mrs. Drake's native tongue, and therefore did not know that what Mrs. Drake had said in Visayan translated to 'fuck your eyes' in English, she pretty much knew she'd just been insulted by Mrs. Drake's tone.

"Get your little fuckin' foreign ass outt'a here and don't come back!" Karen yelled. "You're banned!" And already, Karen was adding another five K to next month's paycheck, because she was hoping the woman in front of her didn't understand English enough to know what it meant to be banned, and that she would return again before Christmas.

"Pesti mata, ka!" Mrs. Drake said, again, as she turned to go. She knew exactly what Karen had meant, and she knew exactly what she was going to do about it.

Mrs. Drake left the post office and got into her car, but she did not leave. She waited, and she watched, and at noon, after

Karen had locked the post office up for lunch and gone to her own car, Mrs. Drake followed her.

Karen drove up the road, heading away from C'ville, and she stopped at a roadside shithole, one of the few in the area, and she went in to have a beer and a burger and another beer for desert. She had not locked her car, allowing Mrs. Drake to slip something under the driver's seat. Just a little trinket, one would think, if they were to find it. Part of a coconut husk. A coconut husk that had been treated with a special potion and then allowed to burn.

Unknown to anyone who might view it as a trinket…

… a fully cocked and loaded weapon!

But not a bomb.

Unless, of course…

…you considered it to be…

A Bigfoot Sasquatch bomb!

***

Karen made it back to the post office after having one for the road after desert, three beers total, and she finished out her day relatively uneventful. A beautiful young lady, one of the local college girls, Karen assumed, came into the post office to mail something out with less than a minute before close, and Karen was about to go up one side of her and down the other, but she didn't. She hesitated. This beautiful young lady looked familiar.

"Do I know you?" Karen asked.

"I don't think so," the girl said, but her facial expression said differently. She squinted her eyes a bit and turned her head sideways, trying to recall where *she* might have seen *Karen* before.

Karen looked at the return address on the envelope the girl had handed her. The girl's name was Jane. She then looked at the receivers address and noted that it was going to a location familiar to her back in Appalachiastan.

Karen realized she *did* recognize the girl. She was that crazy bitch from the next town over from Karen's hometown back in Appalachiastan who was rumored to have killed off several men. Only rumors, however, as Jane had never even been *questioned* in any of the disappearances. Also, Karen remembered, Jane's town was infatuated with tales of Bigfoot Sasquatch and all kinds of other weird beliefs.

"Fifty cents," Karen said, deciding not to get any friendlier with this beautiful young lady than she did anyone else. Jane handed Karen two quarters then turned to leave.

"Fucking hillbilly," Jane said as she exited the post office, having recognized Karen. She knew where she'd seen her before. She'd gone back to Appalachiastan to show one of her privileged white friends from college, her roommate and a real Karen, how the other half lived some time back, and she'd seen fake Karen out delivering mail when she'd almost reached home. She was from the next town over from hers, Jane remembered.

"Fucking hillbilly," fake Karen said, watching Jane drive off as she, Karen, locked the door to the post office behind her. She was done for the day and it was time to go home and get shitfaced. Karen, though only having been with the post office just over a year now, had already succumbed to the typical lifestyle of far too many postal workers. Go to the job you hate that makes you miserable by day, then go home and get shitfaced drunk and pass out by night. Wake up the next day and repeat the process. Except for on Sundays and Federal holidays. On Sundays and Federal holidays you just get shitfaced all day. No work.

But hey, at least after thirty years you get a pension! And that pension meets sixty percent of your financial needs! So you only have to work part time in order to survive!

More time to get shitfaced!

One of the things that sucks most in life, Karen thought, as did any true alcoholic, was catching that three beer buzz at lunchtime and then feeling it wear off over the course of the next hour. This feeling sucked. Karen, having had experienced this today, decided she'd take a shortcut to her urban housing development in Charlottesville. There was a back road that weaved its way through one of the rich people areas that she could take and it would save her seven minutes. Why, Karen thought, she could chug a beer in that amount of time. So, instead of staying on the main road on her way into town, she took the shortcut just past the train tracks and began weaving her way down the dark, winding road. With the winter solstice only days away, it got dark early this time of year, and it was already dark now.

"Huh," Karen said, peering through her windshield about a mile down the old backroad. Snowflakes were beginning to fall. Though everyone was up to their assholes in snow back in Appalachiastan the climate was much more mild where she lived now and this was actually the first time she'd seen it snow for the year.

As Karen was admiring the snow hitting the windshield, as well as all the beautifully decorated mansions and estates she was passing- Christmas lights and lit wreaths and artificial deer covered in lights in many of the lawns- she noticed a peculiar smell inside her car. "What the fuck is that?" she said aloud, taking a deep whiff through her nose.

Karen looked down for just a minute, as she surmised that the smell was coming from the driver's well. For an instant, she thought maybe she'd stepped in dog shit, even though the odor wasn't quite that rank. As she looked back up, she saw more than just snow on the other side of the windshield. There, standing in the middle of the road, just as Karen was about to enter a very sharp turn, stood, what she at first thought to be a man, but was not. It *was* something man*like*, but it was much larger than an actual man. Much, much larger.

Karen screamed and cut the wheel hard to the right, sending her car off the road and straight into the front field of one of the local estates. She'd been wearing her seatbelt, so though her car had come to an abrupt halt once it had gone about twenty yards off the road and into the field, where it became engulfed in a mushy soft portion of the property owner's lawn- a low part where standing water stood for long periods of time after any amount of rainfall- she had not been hurt.

"What the fuck was that?" she asked herself as she turned the car off and took off her seatbelt to get out. She hadn't even tried to back out of the lawn, because though she might be dumb, she was not stupid. She wasn't getting out of this predicament without a tow. She knew the best she could hope for would be to flag someone down, and the later it got, the less likely that would be possible, with less traffic on the road and all, so she decided to get out quickly and get back to the road. She was not concerned about the large, upright standing creature she'd seen in the road before her accident, because she was already convinced it was merely a shadow or sorts. Or a spot in the road that had recently been patched, hence a darker shade of pavement at that particular spot than the rest of the road surrounding it. That was so common back in Appalachiastan, where most of the old country roads were pure shit, because there was not enough of a tax base to pay for them to be kept up, unlike the roads here in Albemarle County, Virginia, where there was a huge tax base due to all the wealth. Hell, the Virginia Department of Transportation paved these roads every three years just so the locals who paid more money in taxes each year than the average American earned in a year could see where some of those tax dollars were going.

"Help!" Karen yelled as she reached the road. A car was coming, and as she waved her arms while yelling, she was happy to see that it was slowing down. "I've gone off the road," Karen said as the car that had been coming pulled up beside her and came to a stop. The driver had already rolled down the window.

"Wait a minute," the driver of the car, a middle aged white woman said. "Don't you work at the post office down the road?"

"I do," Karen said, smiling.

"Go fuck yourself, cunt!" the driver said, and then she put the petal of her Saab to the metal and left Karen in her dust.

"Fuck!" Karen said. However, she didn't revel in her misfortune for long, as the sound of breaking twigs, as if someone or some*thing* was walking in the forest behind her caught her attention. She turned suddenly and stared into the darkness. "Hello?" she said. "Anyone there?"

She heard the sound of footsteps in the dark again, and they sounded closer, but they came to an abrupt halt as the headlights from another vehicle came up the road from the same direction as the last car. Karen began waving her arms, and once again, this car pulled up beside her, it's window down.

"I ran off the road…" Karen began.

"Go fuck yourself, bitch!" the older gentleman in the car said, having recognized Karen from the post office before she'd even finished speaking, and as quickly as he'd stopped, he sped away in his Mercedes Benz, leaving Karen to her predicament.

"Fuck!" Karen said as the Benz' tail lights made their way around the bend.

Snap!

It was another twig snapping, and the sound had come from right behind her.

Karen turned, very slowly, as she could sense the presence of someone or some*thing* standing behind her, and once she'd turned around, she looked straight into the chest of something huge and hairy. Karen began moving her head and her eyes upward, and once reaching a height of about eight feet, she looked into the eyes of…

Bigfoot Sasquatch!

The Bigfoot Sasquatch that stood only a foot away from Karen let out a mighty roar of anger as it raised both fisted hands high into the sky and then brought them both down with the force of a sledgehammer, bashing Karen on top of the head. The blow had not *killed* Karen, but it had knocked her the fuck out. After she fell, the beast picked her up, flung her over its (or his, or her) back, and vanished into the woods just as mysteriously as it had crept out of them.

Karen was never seen or heard from again.

***

Local Sheriff's deputy Burt Reynolds would end up being the lead investigator into the disappearance of a local postal clerk, but his investigation would turn up nothing. Karen's car was impounded, and it remained impounded, indefinitely, as none of Karen's next of kin wanted to come all the way from Appalachiastan to claim it. When they'd been contacted and informed of Karen's disappearance, their response had been "Hm." When asked if they'd seen her, all of her relatives stated, "no. But if *you* do, tell her she still ain't welcome around here." Reynolds had no idea what that meant, but he'd known a few folks from Appalachiastan and he'd always noted how so many of them seemed to completely hate their entire families.

Reynold chalked Karen's mysterious disappearance up to the same unexplained phenomena he'd been chalking so many recent disappearances and deaths in the area up to.

The unexplained.

But in his heart, he knew the truth.

Sure, he thought to himself. He could go out and question Dr. (honorable) Drake some more, about that whole Bigfoot Sasquatch thing, but he was sure he'd pretty much get the same response from the man that he'd gotten last time- the time he found those two smoking hot Asian girls who weren't really Asian standing in the middle of the road, in the same part of the county as Karen's recent disappearance, wearing U.S. flag embroidered bikinis and geisha gowns with make-up running down their beautiful faces.

"Was she a bitch?" Drake would ask. "That's what most people thought," Reynolds would say. "Then you know what happened," Drake would respond, and then he'd take back up whatever book he'd been reading when Reynolds had shown up, unannounced, dismissing Reynolds without formally dismissing him.

"Maybe I'll go see him after the new year," Reynolds said to himself while leaving the sheriff's office for the day and heading home to enjoy a couple of days off. He was looking forward to putting up the Christmas tree with his family. He smiled at the thought, thinking of how he and his teenage son were finally spending more time together. Then, thinking of actually taking some of that time away from his son, and his wife, for that matter, to investigate the disappearance of a miserable, disgruntled degenerate that no one in the area seemed to like, anyway, knowing what the end result would be, anyway, he had another thought.

Maybe not!

The End

2

Snow Angels

Carolyn was forty now, and she couldn't figure out why she was so unhappy. Especially on this day. The day after Thanksgiving. The day that she and her husband Tom, and their two beautiful daughters, Ella and Jenna, were putting up and decorating the Christmas tree.

Tom was taking the easy way out, as he'd begun to do in recent years. At forty two years old, Tom was feeling tired these days, and he was taking full advantage of his sales skills by sitting on the couch and watching his girls, as he referred to his wife and daughters, do all the work.

"I *am* working," he'd told them when they'd adamately admonished him for his lazy ways. "I'm supervising." And to prove it, every now and then, between sips of ale, he'd tell one of his daughters, or Carolyn, that the left side of the tree had far more ornaments than the right side, and to make sure to place their next few ornaments on the right side of the tree to even it out.

After hanging every third ornament or so, Carolyn would stand back and take it all in. Her girls- Ella ten years old now and Jenna eight- were so adorable, she thought. They'd both gotten the best genes that she and Tom had to give. They were already dominating all the other kids, including the boys, in any and all sports they played. Carolyn wasn't surprised, and it was due to those aforementioned genes. She and Tom had met while competing together on the track team back in college.

And Tom, Carolyn thought. So handsome, despite his middle aged spread. Sure, he still jogged and ate mostly healthy, but the occasional six pack (or twelve) of beer and four slices of pizza at a time a couple times a month (or week) contributed to the stereotypical *dad bod* so many men his age sported.

But through it all, his ever growing belly and all, Tom had always been faithful. He'd always been supportive. He had always been loving to both Carolyn and his daughters.

Carolyn, herself, had done everything the way she was supposed to do it. She never got in trouble in school, avoiding any negative marks on her proverbial *permanent record* that people never figure out doesn't *really* exist until they hit forty. Her grades and athletic achievements had gotten her into college, where she'd graduated cum laude, just like both of her parents before her. Yet, and like so many middle class yuppie types with whom she fully identified, she felt as if having done everything the right way was one big recipe that led up to nothing more than a feeling of emptiness. It's like, it had all been one big lie. At times she actually felt regret for never having been more daring- taken a risk- gotten arrested, even- just to see if having strayed down the proverbial *wrong road* for a while may have added more spice to what she felt was her extremely boring perfect life.

Carolyn thought more of her past as she watched Ella and Jenna struggle over the star for the top of the tree. Tom, just like last year, would have to get up off his rump and help them with this part of the project, putting an end to his supervisorial ways.

What was coming to Carolyn's mind now was the ten years she'd spent teaching before getting pregnant with Ella and making the decision to stop working and stay at home to be the best full time mommy she could be. Tom was pulling down six digits pretty easily at his brokerage firm by then, and they'd never lived above their means, unlike many of their middle class yuppie type peers who were so far in debt they'd never get out, so they believed they'd be able to make it off of one income, and for the last ten years they had.

Carolyn knew she had lived the poster image of a life the way it was supposed to be lived. She had everything in life that any non-materialistic/consumeristic yuppie (rare as they are) could want. A beautiful and healthy family. A wonderful home in which to live. Her bills were paid and there was more than plenty of money left over afterward. The only debt she and Tom had was the mortgage, and it was less than half the amount it had started out to be, and Tom's financial prowess had allowed them to accumulate a sizable nest egg.

So why did she feel so empty?

Her mother, God rest her soul, now gone these past three years, had labelled it psychosis immediately after *the event*, as that night when Carolyn had been ten years old, her daughter Ella's age, would always be referred to in hushed tones by Carolyn's parents and doctors. A night and an event of which to this day even her husband Tom was unaware. She would certainly never tell her daughters. This was one of those 'take it to the grave' type things.

A couple of years after *the event*, Carolyn's father, an actual psychiatrist- not the armchair kind, like her mother- would label Carolyn's condition depression. And in order to keep all things ethical, he would send her to see his best good buddy in the business, and his best good buddy, per the orders of Carolyn's father, of course, would put her on a steady stream of meds.

Carolynd never liked the meds. She couldn't stand the side effects. She'd go on and off of them, back and forth, over and over, but her father always figured it out, and he would make sure to witness her taking the pills and he would ground her indefinitely until she could be trusted to self administer. This went on for a number of years, until one day, Carolyn discovered running.

It came first out of anger. Having been caught not taking her pills again and, being fifteen and hormonal and refusing to take them despite her mother and father's demands, she'd ran out of the house, and, well, she'd just kept running.

Carolyn's parents, having decided Carolyn might *not* be coming home after having given her what they'd felt was ample time to cool down, had jumped in the car and gone looking for her and they discovered her four miles down the road from their house. She was standing at the side of the road, hands on her hips, though not bent over. She was standing tall, having already caught her breath, and she wore only a slight glisten of sweat on her face.

"How did you get here so fast?" her father asked, after rolling down the window.

"I ran," she said.

"Want a ride home?" her father asked, the sound of amazement in his voice. Carolyn took his tone as a complement of her achievement and she got in the car and went home with her parents.

As it was, it just so happened to be a month into the new school year. Carolyn's father made a deal with Carolyn that day on the way home in the car. He'd read study after study which proved that long distance running was as effective in treating certain mental illnesses as was many medications. He told Carolyn that if she joined the cross country team at her high school, and if the running seemed to work in her case, then she could quit the meds. Carolyn agreed, and after her father successfully convinced the cross country coach to allow Carolyn to join the team even though they'd started the season two weeks before, the deal was struck. Carolyn got off the meds and she would end up being an all state runner that year as a sophomore, having had no running experience other than the time she'd set out in an angry rage and ran four miles nonstop, mind you, in blue jeans and shoes that, though casual and sporty in nature, were not running shoes.

Caroly's senior year in high school, she was state cross country champion, and she would win the two mile state championship as well in track and field and finish second in the mile. A'la college scholarship, a'la meeting her husband Tom on the college track team, and a'la everything else ever since.

Until a year ago.

When she'd broken her ankle.

Carolyn had been running a 5K fun run, with her daughters, pacing them, when she'd come down off the side of a sidewalk the wrong way, shattering her ankle instantly, and then falling to the ground and writhing in pain.

Her running days, at least for the foreseeable future, were over.

About three months after her injury, Carolyn began slipping into what her father (and God rest his soul, too, as he'd died a year before her mother) had referred to as depression way back when. Carolyn knew it. She knew the signs well. However, she could remember the side effects of the meds, and she refused to go see a doctor, who she felt would insist she begin taking them again, despite Tom's pleas to get her to make an appointment with someone.

"I'm sure they've come a long way with those things," Tom had told her when he and Carolyn had talked about her blues. He could tell she was down, and he knew most of it had to do with the fact that she'd lost a very important part of her lifestyle-part of who she was, with the loss of her running- and it was only then that Carolyn had confided in him that, as a child, she'd been diagnosed with depression and that she'd been on meds. It was the first time in their more than twenty years together that Tom, a former All-American steeplechaser back in college, truly knew the reason Carolyn had become a runner in the first place. However, she certainly did *not* tell him about the night of *the event*. Oh, no! That one- *the event*- was going with her to the grave.

Even the girls were now noticing Carolyn's long naps and though they never voiced their concern, they did *have* concern over Mommy's drinking. They'd never seen Mommy touch a beer, but a few months after her injury, Mommy started having a beer with Daddy. Now, on more than one occasion, they were finding themselves peeking around the corner of their room and down the hall on nights when Daddy had to carry Mommy to bed because she'd gotten drunk and passed out on the couch again.

"Who's going to plug in the lights?" Carolyn asked as she helped herself to one of Tom's beers, the thought of a beer having popped into her mind. Everyone acted as if they hadn't noticed, and as if they were not concerned, but they had, and they were.

"Me!" the girls yelled in unison, and just like every year in the past, they held the plug and stuck it into the outlet together. The tree lit up brightly, and just like every year in the past, it was absolutely beautiful! Carolyn and her family would no doubt have yet another wonderful Christmas.

Their lives were perfect.

Absolute bliss!

And Carolyn was miserable…

***

Nothing could have made for a more perfect day for putting up the tree than what had happened during the last hour of the day.

Snow!

It was the first snow of the year, and it was coming down now, an hour after dark, hard and heavy. It hadn't come as a surprise, as the weather forecast had been calling for it, but Carolyn and Tom had both warned the girls not to get their hopes up too much, because the forecast was so often wrong. However, the forecast had been right on the money this time.

The couch in the living room was positioned so that when sitting on it, one could either turn their head slightly to the right and see the fireplace, or, turn their head slightly to the left and look out the large picture window. There was no television in the living room of this house. Never had been; never would be. And the family of four had sat on the couch in that last hour of daylight, alternating glances between the fire in the fireplace and the snow coming down outside, and of course, their beautiful tree, which stood in the middle.

The girls had cuddled up between Tom and Carolyn, going on and on about what they wanted for Christmas, now only weeks away. Their parents had teased them about having doubts that they could behave for the final weeks leading into

Christmas, this, as every child knew, a requirement to get what they wanted.

It had been a long, emotional and adrenaline filled day, and it was no surprise to Carolyn that both the girls and Tom dozed off shortly after dark. Carolyn had made her way well past the three beer buzz well *before* dark and she was now well on her way to oblivion. Sure, it would have been the perfect lead in for passing out drunk on the couch, but with the snow, still visible as it came down outside by moonlight, sleep was the furthest thing from Carolyn's mind.

What filled Carolyn's mind at this time, while the most important people in her life slept beside her, was memories, vivid memories of *the event* from all those years ago.

***

Carolyn had been eight years old at the time, the same age of her younger daughter, Jenna, now. It was the same time of year, potentially to the day. Mommy and Daddy were finishing up getting ready for a Holiday party (not a Christmas party, mind you, because Mommy and Daddy's friends were politically correct long before being politically correct was cool- or even a thing, for that matter), and Carolyn had been staring out the window, witnessing the year's first snowfall.

"It's snowing!" she yelled with the excitement only a child could muster for such weather. "It's snowing!"

"Uh, huh," her father had said, tying a tie around his neck. Her mother had chosen to ignore her entirely, as her mother would do most of her life.

Carolyn paid no never mind. She continued staring out the window, and as she did so, she saw the headlights of a car pull into her drive. She stared down from her second story bedroom window, through the windshield of the car in the driveway, and she saw her babysitter, Laurie, leaning over from the passenger seat and kissing her boyfriend, Michael, who had brought her. Carolyn knew that about fifteen minutes after her parents had left, Michael would drive back around and stop, and he would come in, and after Laurie and Michael thought Carolyn was asleep, they would make all those weird sounds they always made down in the living room on the couch. The very sounds that kept her from being able to fall asleep for the longest of times when Laurie came over to babysit. It was as if, Carolyn thought, while lying in bed so many nights listening, after children go to sleep, or at least the adults thought, adults reverted back to the language of primitive grunts and groans for communication, rather than sticking with the actual words used in modern language. Except for the words "oh God," and "I'm coming." That one had *really* thrown Carolyn the first time she'd heard it. To her knowledge, Laurie and Michael had never left.

Mommy and Daddy had given Carolyn kisses and hugs, and Daddy's had been half-heartfelt. Mommys had felt as cold as the snow blowing outside, but that hadn't been new. And then, Mommy and Daddy were off, and within minutes, Michael was pulling back into the driveway. An hour after that, Carolyn was in bed, listening to the 'ooh's' and the 'awe's' and the occasional 'oh Gods,' and after Laurie and Michael had both come back, even though Carolyn had never heard them leave, things got pretty quiet downstairs, but still, Carolyn could not sleep. She was too excited about the snow and the upcoming Christmas that it always brought with it.

Deciding not to even *try* to fight sleep, Carolyn had gotten out of bed and she'd made her way back to the window to watch the snow. However, something was different this time. As she peered out the window, down to the snow covered lawn below, she saw a figure.

At first, she thought there was a man standing at the edge of her yard, just on the lawn side of the treeline that represented the beginning of the forest that stretched for miles beyond her family's property. But as she squinted her eyes and looked closer, she realized this was no man. Men don't get that big, except for those guys that Daddy liked to watch put on those pads and helmets and throw footballs around to each other on Sundays. But even those guys looked small in comparison to the figure she now saw on her lawn.

Carolyn watched, in awe, as the figure moved further away from the treeline and closer to her house. It was standing in the middle of the lawn when all of a sudden it flopped down on its back and it began, of all things, making snow angels.

Carolyn laughed, and she put her hand over her mouth, realizing how loud she'd been. She had the feeling that Laurie and Michael were asleep downstairs, both now having come back from never having left, and she didn't want to wake them. She laughed again, more quietly, but somehow, the figure on her lawn seemed to have heard her. It stopped it's flapping motion and lifted its head. It peered up, as if looking right into Carolyn's eyes, like it could somehow see in the dark, and then, it waved.

Carolyn, with the innocence of a child, waved back, convinced she was looking at a bear or some silly circus animal that had been highly trained and then had escaped, having been a bit *too* highly trained. Whatever the case, and whatever it was, she did not fear it. She watched it play in the snow, and she giggled at its antics, and she acted scared when it formed a snowball in its giant hands, or paws, as Carolyn saw it, and threw it in her direction, but even then she wasn't *really* scared. And when it waved for her to come down and join it? She had no reservations, and she did.

Carolyn had sneaked downstairs, and she had sneaked right by Laurie and Michael. They were both sleeping on the couch, without their clothes, and Carolyn could never understand why they seemed to get so hot every time they came over, but she did her best to cover her eyes as she made her way past them and to the backdoor, which was actually on the *side* of the house. She then made her way out onto the lawn to join the silly circus animal that had obviously escaped and had ventured out to play in the snow. She'd slipped her coat and snow boots on just before going out. She'd had them both by the door in the hopes it would, indeed, snow.

When Carolyn reached the creature standing in her yard, she stared straight up and into its face. She'd never seen anything so tall. Anything that stood on two legs, of course. The creature was covered with hair and it looked like no circus animal Carolyn had ever seen, but just before she might have gotten scared, for real, considering what the creature before her might be, the creature smiled and it giggled and Carolyn did the same, and in unison, as if reading each other's' minds, they fell to their backs and they began making snow angels.

Carolyn and her new, strange friend played for hours. Sure, it was cold, but when Carolyn would shiver, her new, strange friend would pick her up in its warm, harry arms, and it would warm her. It would give her hugs that were *not* half-heartfelt, and certainly not cold. For the first time in her life, Carolyn felt loved.

How could this be? Carolyn could remember thinking, even years later, and even as an adult. *How could I feel so loved and accepted by something not even human that didn't know me any better than I even knew what the hell it even was?*

Carolyn, at one point during a college psychology 101 class would hear the term 'empath' and she would instantly think back on the night of *the event,* but just as the professor said the idea of 'empathy' could not be scientifically proven and therefor was nothing more than a myth- a psychological superstition- she'd written the idea off just as quickly as it had entered her mind. After having felt found for half a second, she once again felt lost.

But not on the night of *the event.* Oh, on that special, snowy night Carolyn had felt loved and accepted for the first time in her life, and she had had so much fun playing with her new friend, and it mattered not to her what sort of animal it might be. It was her new companion, and with her new companion she made snow angels. She built a snowman. She and her new companion threw snowballs at each other and a few at Michael's car. They were doing all the things that Mommy and Daddy had never made the time to do with her, and after having done these wonderful, wonderful things for some time, and Carolyn having caught cold again, her new companion picked her up in its arms and hugged her, for real, and warmed her…

…and then they were hit right in the face with blaring headlights!

Mommy and Daddy had just pulled into the drive, and they'd seen Carolyn and her friend.

"Let my daughter go!"

It was Daddy's voice. Without even turning the car off, he'd jumped out and had begun running into the yard, through the snow, toward Carolyn and her new friend.

Carolyn's new friend put her down, kissed her lightly on the head, and as if it had never been there at all, it disappeared into the treeline…

…never to be seen again.

***

Daddy had thought of calling the police on the night of *the event*, but after having gone back to the car to get a flashlight in order to see which way the perpetrator had fled, based upon his (or hers or its) tracks, and having seen the tracks left behind, Daddy did *not* call the police. Further, Daddy had instructed Carolyn and Mommy that no one was to *ever* speak of the event. *EVER!* And *the event* was certainly never to be spoken of in the presence of others, because there was *no way* the good psychiatrist would be labelled crazy. Why, it would cost him his business and his family their livelihood.

Daddy, or course, would spend the rest of Carolyn's childhood trying to convince her that *she* was crazy. She had not, he would tell her when she broached the subject, played in the snow, for well more than two hours, with something that does *not* exist. She, he would tell her, was so fortunate not to have been kidnapped by some psychotic lunatic child molestor who had obviously been out on that dark, snowy night, seeking his next victim. Carolyn, her father would go on to put the proverbial icing on the cake, had been one lucky little girl.

But Carolyn had always known the truth.

And never having spoken of it, aloud, to anyone, her entire life, had driven her into a very painful, lifelong depression.

As now forty year old Carolyn reminisced about the night of *the event* when, then *eight* year old Carolyn had had the time of her life, playing in the snow with something that was not supposed to exist, and of how innocent and wonderful it had been- the complete opposite of having to bury the lie of *the event* and the creature's existence for the next thirty two years of her life- she was brought back to the present time and present events by way of noticing a large, dark figure standing just outside the treeline, in her yard, where the lawn bordered the forest.

Could it be?

"I'm seeing things," Carolyn said to herself, softly, as she rose, ever so carefully, making sure not to wake her family. She then made her way to the large picture window and stared out into the snowy darkness for a better look.

"Oh, my God," she said. Either her eyes were deceiving her, or she was shitfaced drunk, she thought, because she was still seeing what appeared to be standing by the edge of the forest.

Carolyn, as quietly and stealthily as she'd gotten off the couch and made her way to the picture window slipped out the front door of her family's home and into the dark, snowy night. She hadn't put on her coat, and she wore only houseshoes on her feet. She was wearing flannel pajama pants and an old Nike hoodie that was ragged and worn and because of both factors, more comfortable than anything else she usually wore around the house. It was cold, but she was well into her cups, so she wasn't feeling the effects of the weather, and besides, her focus was not on the temperature, but on the figure she believed she'd seen at the edge of the woods.

Just as Carolyn made her way out of the realm of light being cast onto the snow from within her house out of the picture window, and into the shadows, the figure she believed she'd seen appeared to have ducked into the woods. Carolyn decided to follow.

Carolyn made her way fifty yards or so into the woods before the effects of the weather and the temperature really hit her, and in a word, sobered her up. She realized she was cold, she realized she was out in the snow, and in the woods at that, and in what she referred to her outfit as her 'skivvies' and wearing only house slippers. She realized that the creature that she thought she'd seen could not have been real. Sure, it might have been real all those years before, when she'd seen it as a little girl, but what she was experiencing now was merely what her parents might have referred to as an episode of psychosis. Mostly alcohol and memory induced.

Carolyn was convinced she'd finally lost all her marbles, and that she was now completely, indefinitely, totally and undeniably, batshit crazy.

Carolyn stood, figuratively staring over the precipice of her insanity, at a spot in the forest where there was a wide opening in the canopy above her. The moon was full and its light shone down brightly through the opening in the canopy above her. She looked up, through the tree tops and to the moon, and she said, "fuck it. What the fuck is it all for, anyway?"

With that, she fell flat on her back, she made several snow angels, and then, and for the last time, she hoped, she fell asleep.

**

"Daddy!"

It was Ella. She'd woken up to find that Mommy was gone, and she was scared.

"What is it?" Tom said, waking and sitting upright, rubbing tired eyes.

"Mommy's gone!"

"There she is," Jenna said. She'd woken up when her sister had woken their father. She hadn't even noticed her mother was gone. She'd simply run to the picture window to see if it was still snowing.

Tom and Ella rose from the couch and they made their way to the window. They joined Jenna in staring out of the window and what they saw shocked them all. Jenna had been right. There was Mommy.

Outside.

Being carried!

Someone, or some*thing*, was carrying Mommy, limp in its arms, from out of the forest. Just as it reached where the light cast through the window met the darkness, it knelt, and it ever so gingerly lay Mommy in the snow. Then, it stood, it turned, and it slowly made its way back into the forest.

"What in the name of God?" Tom said, just a whisper.

"Go get her, Daddy," Ella said. "Before that bear comes back."

Tom knew that what had carried his wife out of the forest and lain her on the snow covered lawn was certainly no bear, but he did agree that it would be best for him to retrieve his wife and bring her into the house before it, whatever in God's name it (or he, or she) was, returned, and he did.

When Tom brought Carolyn into the house he carried her straight to their bedroom and put her in bed. She slept the rest of the night, the alcohol running through her veins a big help. When she woke up the next morning, fortunately with no hangover, she believed she'd had a very vivid dream, brought on, no doubt, by a combination of the time of year, the snow, the booze, but mostly, memories of *the event* from all those years ago.

However, Tom and the girls, after allowing Carolyn plenty of time to wake up over coffee, informed her that the events of the night before had not been a dream. They had been real.

Very real.

Carolyn's family decided they'd keep the events between themselves. However, unlike her parents when she'd been a child, they decided that they could and would speak of the events, amongst themselves, as freely and as often as they liked.

Carolyn found immediate comfort in being able to talk about things no one else would ever believe with the people who mattered to her the most. She found comfort in knowing she was not crazy, and she found comfort in no longer having to live the lie.

Carolyn gave up drinking as a New Year's resolution a little more than a month later. By the following spring, her injury had healed to the point that she could begin running, lightly, again, and by fall she was running local 5K's and 10K's again.

And every Christmas, while families all over the world stare out their windows, waiting on a fat man in a red suit who is said to ride around the entire world, giving gifts to all the children of the world, Carolyn and her family stare out their big picture window waiting to catch a glimpse of something else. Something as reclusive, if not more so than the man they call Saint Nick. They wait, sometimes patiently, sometimes not, to see if they can capture just a glimpse of…

…potentially…

…Bigfoot Sasquatch!

The End

3

Look What The Cat Dragged In

"So far, so good," Robert said to Nick, leaning up against the small table that worked as a counter. Nick had just rung up another satisfied customer, the new, proud owner of a six feet tall spruce tree they'd paid Nick and Robert sixty hard earned dollars for, but for which Nick and Robert only paid only ten, having bought an entire tractor trailer load's worth from a Christmas tree farm in Pennsylvania. Sure, Robert and Nick had nearly a thousand trees planted on their property, a beautifully lain out five acres homestead in Greene County, Virginia, which sat in a small valley just below the Blue Ridge Parkway- the two of them could almost see their place while driving across the Parkway during the winter months once the leaves had fallen from the trees- but it was the trees they bought in bulk, at deep discount, and had trucked down to their Christmas tree farm in Virginia where they made the majority of their profit.

"We're killing it," Nick said. "As long as we don't have any problems."

"We never have before," Robert said, a hushed tone.

"Yeah," Nick said. "But there's never been as many sightings as there has been this year."

"These things are afraid of humans," Robert said. "I'm sure there's not one within miles of us, what with all these people we've been having come out."

"One can hope," Nick said, and then quickly put on his big, plastic smile as he saw another smiling family coming toward the register, the patriarch of which carried another six feet tall spruce. When Nick thought of the fifty dollars profit the tree was about to bring, his fake smile became real.

Robert and Nick had moved to Virginia from New York twenty years before. They hadn't been old when they'd made the move, only early forties at the time, but they knew old age was coming and both of them had been getting less tolerable of the cold, New York winters, which had seemed to be getting colder and more tolerable as they aged.

"Let's move to Virginia," Robert had suggested after having driven down to spend a weekend with an old college pal in Charlottesville.

"Are you serious?" Nick said. "They'll lynch us!"

"Not if we stay close to Charlottesville," Robert had told him. "It's a really progressive area."

"In Virginia?" Nick said, not believing what he was hearing. "A progressive area in the South?"

"It's technically not the South," Robert had told him. "It's the Mid-Atlantic, but you're not supposed to tell the locals."

The two of them laughed, and then after a week spent together in Charlottesville, with Robert's old college pal being their guide, their plans were made and ninety days later, Robert and Nick closed on a five acre tract of land that had a beautiful, antebellum home on it which had been built in 1840, just outside of Charlottesville, and they became two progressive liberals from the northeast who were unknowingly playing a small part in an unforeseen big role or turning the historic red state of Virginia blue. The two of them had fixed the old house on their new land up nicely with the profits from the sale of their apartment in New York, and with the rest, they'd invested in their Christmas tree farm.

"The trees we actually plant and grow are not where we'll make our money," Robert had explained to Nick, understanding the business a bit because he'd had an uncle back in Maine, where he'd grown up before moving away to New York for college and then having stayed for fifteen years after graduating, who had owned and operated a Christmas tree farm. "The trees we'll be planting will be merely for ambience. And we'll have plenty of people who will come just for the experience of harvesting their own tree. But the real money is in wholesale retail. We can get nearly a ten times markup by buying in bulk."

Nick had taken Robert at his word. It had been Robert who'd come up with every business idea the two of them had pursued since having met at a rave and then having had the most passionate night of what had been meant to be one night stand sex either had ever had, and then shaking up together within weeks, having decided the chemistry they had between them was too strong to be used up in only one night. And every business idea Robert had suggested and which they'd pursued had always been profitable. As it would turn out, the

Christmas tree farm idea would be yet another of Robert's wonderful and successful ideas. And now, nearly thirty years after having met at the now long defunk rave (cocaine and the advent of a mysterious virus… and not covid... that would wreak havoc on their community closed down most of the raves), here the two of them were, living happily ever after on their five acres Christmas tree farm in the middle of a state which had been red when they'd come, but which they'd helped turn blue, but neither of which mattered to them now, because all of their tree sales converted to green, pun intended. Oh, and they only had to work six weeks out of the year. From the day after Thanksgiving until Christmas Eve. And even then, only Friday through Sunday, from 10:00 a.m. until 5:00 p.m.

"Excuse me," a severely hungover thirty-ish year old man asked, walking, almost painfully, toward Robert. Robert had made his way back into the field where he and Nick grew their white pines. Most were between four and six feet tall now, but there were many that were only a couple of feet tall, having only been planted either this spring or last, and there were the occasional ten to fifteen footers that were the result of the trees not even having been close to perfect looking saplings in their youth that had never been sold. Robert, always keen to spot economic opportunity, always donated these tall, ugly, gangly giants to churches and municipalities and was more than happy to take the tax write-offs from doing so. "Do you have any saws?"

"Sure," Robert said. He had two limb saws in his left hand, and he had one in his right. He handed the man the one in his right. "Here alone?" Robert asked, his hopes high.

"No," the man said. "My wife and kids are here." And just as he'd finished speaking, his beautiful, not hungover wife appeared, carrying a one year old in her arms, and with a three year old and a five year old following behind her. The children were all boys.

"Have fun," Robert said, turning away from the family, immediately, to dismiss them. It wasn't, however, just because he'd just found out that the younger man was straight and married. It was in order to do yet another safety check of the treeline which bordered his and Nick's property. Their five acres consisted entirely of fields, and their neighbors' properties to the south and the east were fielded properties as well. However, to the north and west? All forested. This was the direction of the Blue Ridge Mountains and the Blue Ridge Parkway. The direction from which all the sightings had occurred, and the direction in which if one were to get lost, they might not be seen again. And not because the area between Robert and Nick's homestead and the distant Blue Ridge Parkway was so vast. It wasn't. It was merely a six mile hike up to the Parkway. It was, however, due to what lived and hunted within that six mile patch of forest that could lead to one's disappearance.

***

"You guys are actually going to stay open until Christmas Eve, huh?" Emerson Eckles said, sipping his complimentary cup of hot cocoa. He was leaning up against the table that Nick used as a counter. Robert had made his way back to the register area after having walked a loop around the planted trees and having seen nothing alarming. Eckles, the local Game Warden, had stopped by as he'd been doing twice a day since the happy, aged couple had opened shop for the season.

"We've made it this long," Robert said. "We've only got ten days to go. I think we'll be fine."

"I hope so," Emerson said, taking another sip of his cocoa. "You know, 'ol Pete Singer over on Pea Ridge saw one of them damn things last week. Said it would'a made off with one of his sheep if he hadn't had his rifle with him and he hadn't shot at it. He'd been out deer huntin'. Perfect timing and situation to see one of them sonsabitches, I guess, if you're gonna see one."

"I don't think we'll have any problems," Nick said, scanning the treelines on the north and west edge of his property with his eyes as he spoke. "Too many people around here. The odor should keep them away."

"Help us! Help us!"

The woman came running and screaming from the field where Robert and Nick grew their white pines. Robert recognized her as the woman that had been with the hungover younger man he'd found attractive, but, unfortunately, also straight and married.

"It got my baby! It got my baby!"

Robert, at first, took the woman literally, seeing that her arms were now empty, but when he saw her good looking and hungover, but unfortunately straight and married husband come running through the trees behind her, he saw that *he* was now holding the baby in one arm, while holding, tightly, onto the hand of the couple's oldest child with his other hand.

But subconsciously, he knew the math didn't add up. Someone was missing.

"It got my baby," the woman said, again, pulling up to a stop at Nick, Robert and Emerson. She saw all three men staring at the actual baby her husband was carrying, and she said, "our middle child! Ryan! He's autistic!"

"What?" Emerson said, dropping his half full cup of cocoa to the ground.

"Ryan," the woman's husband said, now coming to a stop alongside the group. "He's autistic. He just wanders off. All the time. And he did it today."

"I went looking for him," the mother said, "and that's when I saw it. It had Ryan by the nape of the neck, holding him by his coat. And it just trotted off into the woods with him as if he were a doll." She fell to her knees and broke further into hysterics.

"I told you guys not to open up this year," Emerson said to Robert and Nick, beginning to unholster his sidearm while walking away from the group and in the direction from which the distraught family had come. "I'll call backup."

"You fuckers shouldn't have reintroduced the mother fuckers?" Nick said, entirely having lost his cool. "Or you should have at least let the public know about it."

***

Once upon a time, long before white settlers ever stepped foot on the eastern shores of what is now the United States of

America, great predators roamed the eastern forests; large wolves, giant cats, and, potentially (and not to mention according to more than one now non-existent, formerly local indigenous tribes) Bigfoot Sasquatch. These creatures lived in harmony with each other in the wild, fulfilling their duty as an intricate part of the food chain and biosystem. Like most non-herbivorous wild animals, if something was smaller than them, they killed it and ate it, and if something was larger than them, they hid from it or ran from it.

And then the settlers came.

Oh, how these settlers loved particular animals they'd never seen in the old world, like white tailed deer and wild turkeys. Especially when they ate them. But the wolves? The giant cats that weighed more than the white tailed deer? And especially that large, hairy man of the forest? Oh, how these creatures instilled the fear of the almighty God into these settlers, so they did what their kind had done for thousands of years.

They killed them all!

The men of any and all local populations in the new world would ban together, often, and perform what was known as 'circle hunts.' The men would determine how much land they could surround, this being based upon the number of men who'd shown up for the hunt, and then they would form a large, outer perimeter and then hunt their way into the center, killing anything and everything that wasn't human, occasionally, however, killing or severely wounding one of their own, as well, by way of poor and usafe shooting.

As flourishing as many of these large, fierce, wild predators were when the fair skinned settlers first came to this land, by the end of the fair skinned settlers' first century, many of these creatures no longer existed east of the Appalachian Mountains. And, as the fair skinned settlers would work their way west, these creatures would cease to exist east of the Mississippi. Only because these fair skinned settlers, all these centuries later, had no desire to live in large numbers in some of the most uninhabitable conditions (for humans) at the top of the Rocky Mountains or the Cascades in the far and extreme west, do these animals still exist in the continental United States. In just about any and all other terrains with climates suitable for the human condition, these beautiful creatures have been entirely extirpated.

It is said that the last official sightings of the eastern mountain lions took place around the time of the end of the American Civil War. Sure, there have been many folks claim to have seen them, or heard them at night- sounding like women being murdered, screaming from somewhere deep in the forests- since, but those who have made such claims have been summarily written off as crackpots. Many of them, still yet, had heard the cries of foxes or the screeching of screech owls, and had merely never spent enough time in the wild to be familiar with the often terrifying sounds such animals can make.

However, in more recent times, as in, the past two decades, many of the sightings and the reports of hearing strange sounds may have carried more validity. For you see? There has been quite a change in the mindset of those fair skinned settlers' descendants that has caused yet another rift in the biosystem, namely, in the food chain.

Once upon a time, it was highly understood that people's food came from farms. Vegetables were grown, meat came from animals that were raised and slaughtered and then butchered. Everything was packaged up and sold by way of the market, and then later, the grocery store.

So much time has passed, however, since the masses of fair skinned settlers and their descendants lived in any such way that would place them in a situation where they might witness part of this process with their own eyes. With the industrial revolution of the early part of the twentieth century, Americans made a great exodus from the country and the farms, and they flocked to the cities to work in jobs that hadn't existed in times before. As time does, time marched on, and as economies and societies do, both evolved, and for more than a century, the overwhelming population of Americans would live in urban or suburban areas. Farms were something they had sung about in kindergarten, along with all those e-i's and o's. And all the farm animals wore smiles on their faces and loved being scratched behind the ears. And even the grocery stores were now sporting meat neatly packed in packages that bore stickers on the front that said, to the effect, "the animal which provided this meat for your consumption lived in better conditions than eighty percent of the world's human population (and that part was true), and when it was slaughtered and butchered for your consumption, it was only after it had led a nice, long life, and it was in full consent of the process, and the process was only carried out after the animal had naturally expired, and before having expired, of course, the animal had given its full consent to be butchered and consumed by humans, much like organ donors give consent at the D.M.V. (this part was not true- but the masses were convinced).

In a word, the killing of animals (and by the way, the only *safe* word to use in this regard on social media and *not* have your account suspended is "dispatch") for the sole purpose of human consumption had become kin to evil incarnate. Sure, these yuppie types who believed and pushed this tripe still ate meat, but again, meat from animals who'd been petted and loved and blah, blah, blah…

So, here's the point.

Certain wild animal populations, such as the white tailed deer, which had always been properly held in check largely by way of hunting, became overpopulated by the end of the twentieth century. By the end of the first decade of the twenty-first century, there were literally more deer being killed by drivers and cars than by hunters and guns than a generation before. And the damage these out of control deer herds were inflicting on crops? People's gardens, flowerbeds, shrubs, trees, bushes and lawns?

Monumental!

Oh, but how dare the Division of Natural Resources carry out culls to control the herds! This was tried, and all those Karens and whatever you call the beta-males Karens marry came running out of their houses, banging on pots and pans to scare away the cute little sixty eight pound malnourished deer that were in their yard when the Government people came by with their crossbows to *dispatch* them.

It didn't work.

So, what did they do next?

Well, and here's the part you won't hear about…

...they secretly reintroduced the natural predators of such overpopulated, now nuisance animals like the white tailed deer. The very predators their ancestors had extirpated generations before.

They started in remote areas with coyotes; these being the least dangerous wild predator to human populations. Though there is the occasional story of a coyote carrying away a three year old child at least annually, the endings of those stories are relatively positive. The coyote only carries the child a few yards before realizing they're too heavy and then it drops them and then heads for the hills. Coyotes hunt in packs, and they specialize in going after wounded animals, and at first, it was a perfect fit, what with all those wounded white tailed deer limping around after having been hit by Karen in her K-car. However, Karen would in time begin driving priuses. Tiny little half electric cars that would get demolished if they hit a squirrel, let alone a full grown sixty eight pound malnourished deer. And sometimes the deer were healthy and actually weighed a hundred pounds or more. How on earth could a Prius stand up to that?

It couldn't.

Obviously, there was no way to minimize the Karen population, so a way to combat the Karen populations' mindset and lifestyle of privilege and comfort and the utter destruction on the very environment these Karens were claiming to save with their Priuses and reusable shopping bags had to be come up with, so, "they" began introducing even more fierce predators to the scene. Predators like gray wolves and cougars.

But "they" had to be careful here. These animals, if given an opportunity, would attack humans, and they didn't need their pack of buddies, like coyotes (though the wolves preferred it). Especially those cats. The world's most lethal hunters. The only animals that weighed nearly two hundred pounds and measured nearly eight feet in length that could sneak up on the most vigilant human standing in the middle of an empty field without being detected.

But "they" did it.

And the result?

The deer herds began diminishing, which led to less crop damage and less deer induced auto-accidents. People could plant ornamental trees and shrubs in their yards again without having to cage them in with chicken wire to protect them from the deer. And the best part? It all happened out of the range of the eyes and the ears (except for the occasional late night scream from the forest that was overheard by clueless campers, but the DNR could always convince them it had been a fox) of Karen, her beta-male husband, and the children of Karen and whoever she'd cheated on her beta-male husband with to produce said children.

Oh, and…

…well…

Welcome to the Christmas tree farm!

***

"What do you mean, 'reintroduced the mother fuckers?'" the hungover father asked Nick as everyone except Emerson stood by, clueless as to what to do.

"Long story," Nick said, not wanting to tell of everything this writer just wrote. "Things will be okay."

"Okay?" the distraught mother said. "Okay? I just saw my baby get carried off by a mountain lion, and you're telling me everything's going to be okay?"

God, Nick thought. *I'm so glad I'm gay.*

"I'll get the car," Robert said. "Everyone jump in when I pull up, and we'll do what we can."

Robert drove a Toyota Sequoia with a third row of seats, so he, Nick and the distraught family all fit with plenty of room to spare, and once all where in, Robert locked the four wheel drive mechanism and off they went, out into the wild blue yonder, Robert knowing his actions were making the family feel better, but also having the full understanding that there wasn't a goddamn thing anyone was going to be able to do.

In his mind, Nick was weighing the ferocity of the upcoming lawsuit.

***

Three miles away and straight up the steepest part of the mountain, and while Robert was just reaching the edge of his and Nick's Christmas tree farm, with their hysteric and distraught passengers aboard, the mighty, fierce mountain lion eyed a moss covered boulder. This particular boulder was as large as a single story house, and it appeared to butt up against the exposed mountain here as it continued, equally steeply, to the top, another half mile above.

But it did not!

If one were to walk around to the eastward facing side of this large boulder, not only covered in moss but also surrounded with mountain laurel, if they had been fool enough to hike nearly three miles straight up the side of the mountain in the first place, they would notice a crevice where the boulder was disconnected, ever so slightly, from the mountain proper. This crevice measured four feet wide and four feet tall. It was almost perfectly square.

If, persey, one *did* walk three miles straight up the steepest side of the steepest mountain in this part of the Blue Ride, and one *were* to notice the giant boulder covered with moss and surrounded by mountain laurel, and, *further*, should one make their way around to the crevice on the eastward facing side and, out of curiosity, *squat* down and shimmy into the crevice, one would find that just two feet into the crevice, the opening grew wide, and the opening then took a sharp turn northward, heading, by way of tunnel, several hundred feet into the mountain proper. And, at the end of this several hundreds of feet long tunnel, one would find a vast opening, a room for the lack of a better description. And this room, measuring a whopping one hundred feet by one hundred feet served as a home.

And this home, served as a home for…

…Bigfoot Sasquatch!

Bigfoot Sasquatch sat, cross legged, at his (or hers or its, but not their, as there was but one) fire, warming large hands attached by thick wrists on the end of long, strong arms. The hidden cave, which had served as the home for the Bigfoot Sasquatch for some time (in southern terms, that could be from a few seconds to a few millennium, so use your imagination here, and forget that the story is actually taking place in the Mid-Atlantic) never got too cold in the winter, nor did it get too hot in the summer, due to its location hundreds of feet beneath the earth's surface. It was perfectly insulated.

The cave was equipped with running water, as it had an underground stream which flowed through it, conveniently pooling in a perfectly formed hole, created by millenniums of erosion, the size of a bathtub, where enough fresh mountain water to meet long term needs continuously flowed, always providing a great amount, yet due to the continuous flow, always being refreshed.

The smoke from the creature's fire easily and efficiently made its way out of the vast cave by way of literally thousands of tiny openings on the cave's ceiling which channeled through the ground stone, above, like comb of a bee's hive, working like the perfect filter, so that the small amount of smoke given off by the Bigfoot Sasquatch's fires was always absorbed by the soil and stone before even reaching the earth's surface. A hiker could be sitting right on top of the cave, hundreds of feet up through stone and soil and tree roots, and never even smell a hint of smoke coming from the Bigfoot Sasquatch's fire. The cave was the perfect place for creatures that are not supposed to exist to exist.

"Oh, no," Bigfoot Sasquatch thought as the giant cat that had no name came traipsing into the cave, something smaller than itself, yet quite sizable compared to the cat's other previous catches, and fortunately still alive, dangling from its mouth.

"What have you done?" Bigfoot Sasquatch spoke, telepathically, to the cat that had no name. Bigfoot Sasquatch and the cat came from a world that did not use proper names, and as a result, pronouns. Man knew their world as nature, yet though beyond giving it a name, like every goddamn thing else man came across, he respected it little. However, and as they'd honestly admit, due to reasons of self preservation, Bigfoot Sasquatch and his, her, it or their kind respected the world of mankind. They'd (he'd, she'd, It'd) found, throughout time, that it was the best way, nay, the *only* way, to remain undetected, and not become extirpated themselves, if not entirely extinct.

"Tastes good," the large cat with no name said, telepathically, of course.

The language of animals was another area in which man felt he had come so far, yet was so cluelessly unaware. Sure, animals made noises. And many of those noises meant specific things. For instance, in the bird families, this tweet meant, 'hey guys, I found food,' and that chirp meant, 'hey baby, wanna make an eggy?' but the true, meaningful conversations between the animals, even across species, took place telepathically. Even the cavemen had known that, but modern man? Well, to modern man, things had to make sense. Things had to be proven. Without proof, things were not real. So, as advanced as modern man liked to think they were, they were not, and in many ways, this was all the better for the creatures of the fields and the forests.

"We cannot eat their kind," Bigfoot Sasquatch said, telepathically, to the large cat with no name.

"Ah," the large cat with no name replied, telepathically. "Just once?"

(Author's note- henceforth, when writing of the communication between Bigfoot Sasquatch and the large cat with no name, the word *telepathically* will be omitted, as one of Stephen King's (this writer's favorite author) suggestions on writing is to eliminate unnecessary words. This will allow this writer to eliminate up to forty seven unnecessary words. However, always keep in mind throughout this reading, that when these creatures communicate, they are doing so telepathically.)

"No," Bigfoot Sasquatch said.

"Can I keep it as a play toy?" the large cat with no name said.

"No," Bigfoot Sasquatch said. "Take it back."

"Ah," the large cat with no name said. "Do I have to?"

"Yes," Bigfoot Sasquatch said. "Come on," he (or she, or it) said, and together, the two creatures, one of which was not supposed to exist in Virginia, and the other, which was not supposed to exist at all, made their way out of the cave, down the long tunnel, and then they slipped out of the crevice between their hidden passage and the large boulder which camouflaged it, and then they began making their way down the mountain and toward the Christmas tree farm.

***

"What was that!" It was Nick. He was sitting in the second row of the Sequoia's seats. He'd allowed the father of the missing child to ride in front, with Robert (though he'd kept his eyes on Robert, because Robert hadn't always been faithful, and Nick knew Robert had a thing for younger men with drinking problems, often stooping as low as going to AA meetings and picking up men during their first ninety days of sobriety, their greatest time of need, and when they were most vulnerable and easily gotten, even, many of them, if they were straight).

"I saw it!" the father of the missing child said. His hangover had worn off now. It was just after dark. He was really jonesing for a drink, especially with the added emotional strain of the current situation. "Was that a fucking mountain lion?"

"Where's fucking Emerson when you need him," Robert said. "If he was here he could shoot that fucking thing."

"I could have shot the fucking thing twice already if you weren't so anti-gun," Nick said from the second row of seats. Robert chose not to dignify the comment with a response. As much as Robert loved Nick, he would be the first to admit that Nick was a bit of a redneck. But it had always been his alpha, manly ways that had turned him on. And at least he still voted Democrat.

"What the fuck is that?"

This comment stopped all conversation, as it came from five year old Billy who was sitting in the third row of seats.

After everyone turned to look back at the small child who had just dropped a massive F bomb, their mouths agape, they slowly turned their heads, their mouths becoming even more agape, as if it were even possible, as they then stared at, standing dead center in the Sequoia's bright headlights and only twenty feet in front of the vehicle…

…Bigfoot Sasquatch!

And in the arms of Bigfoot Sasquatch, reaching up and tugging at the hair on Bigfoot Sasquatch's chinny chin chin…

…was Ryan. Safe and sound and uninjured.

The group inside the S.U.V. was silent. They could not believe what they were seeing. They remained silent as the Bigfoot Sasquatch in front of them lowered the small child to the ground, let him go, and then slowly walked out of the road and into the woods. A giant cat, one that had no name, because names and certainly not pronouns were used in its world, leaped back across the road, heading now in the direction the Bigfoot Sasquatch had gone, and neither creature was ever seen again.

***

As it turned out, the family who'd been put through the ordeal of having their autistic three year old child taken by a large predator that was not supposed to exist in Virginia chose *not* to sue Robert and Nick. They were grateful to get their child back, unharmed, and they were grateful that Robert had stayed in touch with the patriarch of the family and had actually convinced him to take positive steps (twelve of them, actually) toward combating his drinking problem.

And no, they never got it on, because though Robert strayed from Nick from time to time, the man was faithful to his wife.

And not gay.

The story of what happened at the Christmas tree farm that day never made its way into the media. Had it, Emerson would have done what he'd done a time or two in the past when stories of strange sightings and missing or mutilated livestock *had* made their way into the media.

Deny, deny, deny.

Emerson had been prepared to use the excuse that "distraught mothers' emotions run high and make them see things that aren't there" had the mother of the child gone to the papers (or the shady blogs on the internet) and told her story, but he was grateful it hadn't come to that.

And the story the group had told Emerson about the Bigfoot Sasquatch? Well, he knew there were cougars in the area, thirteen of them for sure, for they were being tracked after having been reintroduced to the wild, secretly, by his department. It was hoped that they were breeding, but his department had still not garnered any evidence that this was the case, yet.

But Bigfoot Sasquatch?

Poppycock!

Those aren't real, and everyone knows it, Emerson thought. Why, modern man has come so far that we know goddam everything! He'd tell you you could even go ask an old acquaintance of his, Jittery J, but Jittery J was dead. "Goddamn, if that 'ol boy didn't know goddamn everything," Emerson said aloud, the thought of Jittery J entering his mind.

And as far as Bigfoot Sasquatch and the large cat that has no name? Well, Bigfoot Sasquatch had a good talking to with that large cat, and that large cat never went anywhere close to where humans resided again, and as a result, was never spotted again.

But that talking to had taken place the day *after* the day of the events that took place on the Christmas tree farm. For you see, on their way home, Bigfoot Sasquatch had received a message. A message transmitted by way of a spell carried out through a burnt coconut husk. A spell cast by a beautiful young Pacific Island woman now as much out of place in Central Virginia as Bigfoot Sasquatch and the large cat with no name themselves.

"You go home," Bigfoot Sasquatch told the large cat with no name (and you remember how they communicate, right? I'm choosing not to use that word for the sake of eliminating unnecessary words, remember). "I'll be home late. I have work."

The large cat with no name headed one way, toward the secret cave, and Bigfoot Sasquatch headed the other. There was a real bitch of a postal clerk about to head home by way of a short cut just a short distance from where Bigfoot Sasquatch now was, but for some reason, a spell had been cast, calling upon Bigfoot Sasquatch's to make sure the woman would not make it home.

Per the final events in the closing paragraphs of story one of this collection…

…she did not.

The End

4

Sisters Of The Secret

I had a best good buddy back in the Philippines. His name was Ray. He was a seventy-ish year old Englishman who thought and lived like he was still in his twenties, and man, did me and that guy have some good times together.

"Why the long face, friend?" were the first words Ray ever spoke to me. But I had no idea what he was saying, because he was speaking in Tagalog, the national language of the Philippines, and it would be quite some time before I'd actually learn to understand and speak the language. I had been sitting at the bar in a hotel restaurant in Manila, the country's capital, having a lukewarm beer (ice seemed to be a precious commodity all over the country, except for at the highly priced five star joints I could not afford to visit) when Ray came in to do the same. It was two o'clock in the afternoon, and aside from the two waitresses who were sleeping behind the counter (they'd given us the go ahead to help ourselves to as much lukewarm beer as we wanted, as long as we left payment on the bar when we left, and asked that we just not wake them) we had the place to ourselves.

I let Ray know I had no clue what he was saying, and since he was pronouncing the Tagalog words with a thick English accent, it sounded like Czechoslovakian to me, anyway, and I doubt I would have understood what he was saying even if I'd spoken Tagalog at the time.

Ray switched over to speaking English, and after I told him my tale- the short version being that I'd gone to the Philippines to meet a girl I'd met online, had been taken major advantages of, had spent twenty 'k' U.S. in three weeks bankrolling her village, and was on my way back to the U.S., my tail between my legs, to nothing waiting on me there- and I explained how I'd recently returned from Iraq to no home, no family, little money. Nothing but problems and people who viewed me as a hero a year before, but a dead-beat embarrassment now.

So much for the short version, huh?

"You got the wrong introduction of the Philippines," Ray informed me. "Have you already bought your plane ticket home?"

"No," I said. "I'm getting it directly from the counter at the airport tomorrow. I don't care how much it costs. This place sucks."

"Give it another two weeks," Ray said. "Come with me to Davao City. Let me show you around. Teach you about the culture, which begins with trusting no one. You can have a lot of fun here. You can meet a lot of beautiful young ladies. And I even know a few who are wonderful. They're not whores and scammers. They're hard working, honest, trustworthy, and did I mention gorgeous?"

"No," I said.

"Well, they are gorgeous," he said. And after more beers than I care to remember, I decided to give it a shot. I did not return to the U.S. at that time. I would go to Davao City, in Mindanao, with my new best good buddy, an ageless man with the wisdom of an old testament prophet, and I would, in time, meet such a girl Ray had described. Actually, Ray is the man who introduced me to her. Her name is Dearly, and she is now my wife, and she was *nothing* like the girl I'd gone to the Philippines to meet (she refused to go out with me for more than a month at first- claiming I talked too much- and she would *never* take *any* of the money I offered her to help her navigate her way through her third world impoverished lifestyle with more ease, no matter how hard I tried to make her take it). When we met, she was in her third year of college and she had a full time job in order to pay her tuition and rent and other living expenses.

Dearly was nothing like any woman I'd ever met in the U.S., either. She was a one of a kind, and after meeting her, I instantly forgot that I was surrounded by thousands upon thousands of the world's most beautiful women who, and I'm just saying it like it is, would jump (and many who *did* jump) at the opportunity to hook up with me, simply because of my skin color and nationality. They viewed me as an instant escape from poverty, and I knew it. They viewed me as a ticket to the U.S. and I knew it. Though they were wonderful people in so many ways, I just couldn't come to terms with the idea of being used for an agenda. But Dearly? Well, like I said, she couldn't stand me and she wanted nothing to do with me nor anything from me, and I was in love with her at first sight, and her lack of an agenda (she said she never wanted to leave the Philippines, let alone travel half a world away to the U.S.) made me want her even more!

So what does this walk down memory lane- a 'how I met my wife' saga- have anything to do with Bigfoot Sasquatch? And Christmas?

Correlations!

My mind works in very mysterious ways, and it draws connections to past events, facts, and theories at times, and this story begins with one of those times.

So, before I met Dearly and began the long process of getting my shit straight (it helped that she actually learned to like me and then love me, and we had a son and came to the U.S. and got married, and have been living happily ever after, etc. etc.) I was a bit of a man whore. This is nothing I'm proud of, but I'm not ashamed, either, as I know I can look back and recognize the fact that I was completely and insanely batshit crazy at that time in my life. And I had somehow ended up in a place where all there is to do, even for the locals, is get drunk and screw. And I spent a hell of a lot of time, as if all the time I was awake, doing both.

"Let me show you how to find some of the most interesting places," Ray said one day while we were walking down the street in Davao City. I'd gone to his apartment bright and early at noon. He'd just finished up his breakfast. Having anticipated my visit, he'd made sure to get up bright and early at 11:00 a.m. and have a slice of toast with coffee before showering and going out with me. This was the beginning of what had been our daily routine for months and would be until I would meet Dearly. Ray had no idea that by introducing me to my future wife he'd end up losing his running buddy.

Ray and I began strolling down what appeared to be a deserted alleyway. (Well, I mean, there were people in the alley, but come on, man, this was the Philippines. There were people everywhere. But for the Philippines it seemed deserted.) The alley made a turn or two, and then it opened up to another barangay (neighborhood) which was located on the beach, and man, what a time we had that day. We visited the barangay's various drinking holes, and got to know quite a few of the local beauties, and ended up discovering what would become one of our favorite places to hang out from time to time, until, of course, I would meet Dearly and change my bad boy ways.

"I've been around the world many times," Ray said as we sat on that white sandy beach, drinking beer that was actually cold, for once, staring out across the Pacific, wondering if we were directly across the ocean from North America or South America. "And what I've found," he continued, "is that most of the greatest treasures truly are off the well beaten path. There are mines with gems, like this place, and like these gems (he nodded his head toward our two companions for the day- two beautiful young ladies in their early twenties who could have and probably would have been pinup models or neurosurgeons had they been lucky enough to enter the world through wombs in the West) all over the place. Most people simply never find them, because they dare not venture off the well worn paths of their lives."

Ray took a big swig of his San Miguel Light, the beer we were drinking and began staring again, across the Pacific. "God, I wish I would have discovered this place when I was your age." He'd spoken the words, and the words before these words like a sex and alcohol addicted Robert Frost, and I was hanging on every one of them.

And then there was Dearly… and then monogamy, and eventually, sobriety, and… well, our homestead in Central Virginia, an S.U.V. driving down an old dirt road our first fall here, enjoying the beauty of the changing of the leaves on the deciduous trees, and a spoiled little boy of five years old sleeping in the back of the vehicle. That was our daily routine back in those days. Our son, Daniel, was in kindergarten. We'd pick him up after school and we'd take one of the various backroads home to look at the leaves and find out more about what was around the area in which we now lived, and, then, on that day, there was…

… a monastery?

Yes, an actual monastery.

""I've been around the world many times," Ray's words from that white sandy beach and all those years ago came to my mind instantly upon seeing something in the middle of the Blue Ridge Mountains of Virginia that seemed so out of place in the middle of this nowhere. "And what I've found," he'd continued that day as we drank cold beer and spent time with young women as beautiful as supermodels, "is that most of the greatest treasures truly are off the well beaten path."

And here was an example of his case in point.

"That's really odd," I commented to my wife. "Who would have thought there would be a monastery out here in the middle of nowhere?"

And then I forgot all about it.

For about two months.

***

Until the morning of election day, 2016.

After I'd voted (I'd gotten there early and was third in line), and I was leaving, I hesitated while opening my car door in the parking lot outside the church that served as our polling station. It was still dark, but I noticed the headlights of half a dozen vans pulling up. They parked by the side of the road, and hordes of nuns stepped out of the vans and went into the church to cast their votes.

"Huh," I said, aloud. "I guess nuns vote."

And then I forgot all about the nuns and their hidden monastery again.

For another three years.

***

Until one overcast afternoon in the late fall of 2019!

I'd been tracking an elusive creature that may or may not have been, potentially, a Bigfoot Sasquatch. The creature, potentially, had been haunting our homestead since long before we'd purchased the land. I mean, I really don't think he, she, it or they showed up just because we moved in. However, this is still a possibility that we've not ruled out, what with our experiences with the Kapre in the Philippines, and whatnot. I sometimes think that cryptids and spirits and all things paranormal and unexplainable attach themselves to those who can see them, and especially, those who can see them and acknowledge them. It's as if, though they don't want to be harmed in any way, nor harm anyone or anything else, they absolutely love the attention of being noticed. And who or what doesn't, right?

Anyway, I'd been pretty heavy into the whole Squatchin' thing for more than a year by this point. And I was taking my camera out into the woods with me on a pretty regular basis and everything, because I'd managed to garner a sizable audience on our YouTube channel, "Homesteading Off The Grid" (ever heard of it?), who were also curious in finding out more about this potential, mythical creature that may or may not exist and which may or may not be living in the woods behind my house. Not to mention, watch to see what sort of ass clown shenanigans I might get up to each episode in my attempts to harness the creature's curiosity bone and pull it far enough out of the woodline to catch a glimpse.

On this particular November day I'd been canvassing a region just outside of an area we've come to call the lair of Bigfoot Sasquatch. It's a location a considerable distance from my home, as far as hiking or driving would be concerned, but not so much as far as the crow flies, or, in this case, the way that Bigfoot Sasquatch travels over hill and dale and mountains and valleys.

All of the leaves from the trees, except for the leaves of the oak trees, had fallen, which gave me greater visibility than usual (the oak leaves fall after Christmas). However, I also knew that this allowed for anyone or anything out there in the forest with me to see me from a greater distance, as well. So, though I could see farther, I was moving much slower than usual, having greater spaces of land in front of me to scope out with my eyes before taking the next steps forward with my feet.

I'd been following what I thought was a large, dark figure that seemed to cloak in and out of our dimension. You see, that's one of the things I've noticed during my cryptozoological explorations. There are times when, and this is not just when viewing things through the screen of my iphone and its, what is often referred to, shitty, archaic 360 uploaded videos, but with my naked eyes, I often see areas in the forest, areas sometimes the size of a man, sometimes a small as a squirrel, where there just seems to be pixelation. I grew up in the mountains of Appalachiastan, and I spent a good portion of my youth in the woods, and I never saw anything like this until I moved to this homestead. Well, except for in the Philippines, on a particular, very creepy island, and, well, I've already hit on this point.

So, on that day, I followed the pixelation. Again, at one point it would be pixelation, and at another it would be a large, dark, blurry object. I'd been following for hours, and I knew I was going to run out of daylight soon, but my curiosity had gotten the better of me hours before, so I continued following. Besides, I'd heard a car or two way down in the valley below me, so I knew there was a road down there, and if I were to get stuck in these woods after dark, my plan was to merely go down to the road and flag a ride. I had been following this pixelated/large, dark, blurry image for too long to give up now.

When I crested the next ridge and stared down over the precipice, low and behold, there was that damned monastery, out in the middle of nowhere. Further, the apparition, if you will, I'd been following, just drifting down the hill, toward the monastery, and once it reached the treeline, where the forest gave way to a large, open field (a field with several nuns tending the past year's garden, I'll add), it formed fully. I stared, in awe and wonder, as what had been pixels one minute, and then a large, dark, blurry image the next, became, in the flesh and fur...

...Bigfoot Sasquatch!

I watched, from a distance of nearly a quarter of a mile, three nuns approach this large, manlike creature. I could not hear what they were saying, but I could tell by their body language that they were speaking. I knew my eyes were seeing what I believed they were seeing, because I was not viewing this scene through naked eyes. I'd taken with me, as part of my potential Bigfoot Sasquatch field research kit (available for purchase, by the way, in our Etsy store, "Homesteading Haven") not only an empty toilet paper roll to use as optics, but one of the long, empty Christmas gift wrapping rolls we'd recently emptied wrapping our son's Christmas presents. It had a much longer range than the toilet paper roll, and I could clearly see the nuns' lips moving as they spoke.

The creature seemed to grunt or growl, or hell, maybe even speak itself. Though I could see clearly through my gift wrapping roll, I was still too far away to hear. And after the exchange, which seemed to last only thirty seconds or so, the creature walked off, but not back into the forest, rather, into a garden that appeared to be walled off with about an eight feet high brick wall. It looked much like the beautiful bricked wall gardens on the campus of the University of Virginia down the road in Charlottesville.

Knowing that which I had been tracking for hours was no longer in the forest with me, I picked up my pace in heading down to the monastery. When I reached the field, the three nuns who'd spoken with the potential Bigfoot Sasquatch approached me, gardening hoes raised over their shoulders as if they were ready to smite me. "You're on private property, pervert!" one of them yelled at me. "You'd best get, or we will eviscerate you!"

"What?" I said.

"That means we'll cut off your balls, you disgusting male creature!" one of the other two nuns said.

"Sisters!"

I turned and saw another nun coming our way. Upon the sound of this nun's voice, the others had lowered their gardening hoes, and I felt my testicles relaxing and dropping back into my scrotum. Instantly, upon having one of the nuns explain to me what 'eviscerate' meant, they'd crawled back up the tubes they'd hidden in until that fateful day puberty would come along and give me body hair in places I'd never had it (and the body odors that came with that), zits, emotional insecurities, and a full sack instead of an empty bag, like many of the local beta-males in my college town who's alpha wives have obviously eviscerated *them* and who have been hiding their jewels in a jar, somewhere, ever since the day they'd been idiots enough to say "I do."

I saw, approaching us, another nun- the nun who had spoken- but she looked nothing like the nuns prepared to turn me into a eunuch. These old biddies had been in their seventies. The nun approaching us, hips swaggering like a goddamn bluejeans model- and yes, this was noticeable despite the black robe she was wearing- was young, much younger. She appeared to be younger than me, even. I was in my mid-forties at the time, and I doubt this woman had hit forty yet. She was in her late thirties at most.

"Put that shit down and get inside," the nun said.

"Sister," one of the old biddies said, under her breath but still loud enough for me to hear, as she passed the much younger, and need I say further, extremely more attractive nun who was still coming toward me. "Your language."

"Shit," the hot nun said. "I forgot." I smiled when this happened, and the hot nun caught my smile and she returned it.

"Lost?" she said when she'd reached me.

"No," I said.

"Then why are you here?" she asked. And by the way, her name was April. I'd find this out, as well as quite a bit more about this hot nun in pretty quick order, but at first, things were a little testy.

"I followed it. Here. All the way from my place."

"Followed what?" April asked.

"You know," I said.

April stared at me hard for a hot second, but then she rolled her head, said, "shit," again, and I could tell, by the way her body, which had been entirely rigid (except for those hips that had sauntered so sexily across the field) until now relaxed, that she wasn't going to play any games.

"Are you alone?" she asked.

"Yeah," I said.

"Do you have a camera? Are you recording?"

"I do have a camera," I said, "and I have been recording. But I'm not now." I pulled my cell phone out of my pocket and showed her that it was off.

"What's that?" she asked, pointing to the empty gift wrapping tube I was holding in my other hand.

"My optics," I said, handing her the tube. She took it from me and held it up to her right eye and she closed her left.

"This doesn't work," she said. "Are you crazy?"

"Maybe," I said.

She looked at me, a very serious look on her face, and then she broke into hysterics and nearly fell to the ground laughing.

"You're a trip," she said. "I would have loved to have done a line with you." She laughed more at that thought.

"A line?" I said. "You mean, like…"

"Yeah," she said. Coke! And not the kind that comes in a bottle."

"Well," I said, warming up to this beautiful, sexy, younger me and not very nunnish nun. "That's never been my thing, but you mention bottle, and well, once upon a time, that was. And, well, I would have loved to have killed a bottle of the top shelf shit with you."

"Oh," she said, regaining her composure. "I can see how *that* would have gone." She stood straight now, pressing the wrinkles that weren't there out of her robe with the palms of her hands. "I would have ended up with *four* illegitimate babies instead of three had that happened."

"Are you serious?" I said.

"You're not gay, are you?" she asked, matter of factly.

"Not that," I said. "I mean, you have three kids?" Then I realized I'd left out an important fact. The answer to her question. So I added it. "And no. I'm not gay."

"Buddy," she said. "Not all of us end up in here because of our love of Baby Jesus." She looked at me in a knowing way. A way that let me know that she knew my mind was blown, quite a feat in internet language, even though we were having this discussion in person. "Not at first," she continued to explain. "But it does come to that. With what people on the outside might call indoctrination. I've come to call it faith. And it's faith based on knowledge."

"How is that possible?" I asked her. "Faith is defined as a belief in things unseen. How can you have actual knowledge of things that have not been seen?"

"The definition does not say unseen by all," she said. "It just says unseen. Some see, some do not see."

She had me. I could relate entirely. It was the reason I'd ended up here in her presence in the first place.

"Speaking of which," I said.

"Ask me no questions, I'll tell you no lies," April said.

"Well, what's up with that?" I asked, wanting the truth, not lies. "I mean, why here?"

"Safe haven," she said. "Sanctuary. They can live in peace and not be hunted."

"They?" I said. "You mean there is more than one?"

"More than one what?" she asked, playing dumb, though smiling coyly, and looking like a naughty-nurse fetish model from an adult website in so doing.

"You've got to give me more than that," I said. "I've been seeing these things on my homestead for the four years I've lived there. I've been tracking them through the forest between here and there for two years now. We finally got one on video, I believe, just last month (this would be the 25 October 2019 video titled "He Discovers The Lair Of Bigfoot Sasquatch And Is Told Loud And Clear He Is NOT Welcome" on our YouTube channel 'Homesteading Off The Grid').

"Where is your homestead?" she asked. I told her, and she said, "give me your cell phone. Let me hold onto it while we're together. I'll drive you home, since it's gonna be dark in, like, five minutes. On the way there, I'll tell you a tale or two, but you are not allowed to repeat what I tell you. And then I'll give you your phone back."

I agreed to her terms, mostly because I didn't want to have to walk home in the dark. It was a long way. I'd been hiking and following what I'd been following all day.

At one point, the thought of my wife getting pissed off and running to the garage to find the machete I keep hidden from her upon seeing me being brought home by a hottie crossed my mind, but I found safety in the fact that the hottie was a nun. Like the majority of people in the Philippines, my wife was a catholic, so she'd recognize the outfit.

On the way home, April told me many things that blew my mind. Not just about that which I'd tracked from my homestead, to the lair, and then to the secret monastery hidden in the middle of nowhere in the beautiful Blue Ridge Mountains of Virginia, but of her own life and her past. As she talked, I did get a flashback to my best good buddy in the Philippines, Ray, and that day he led me down the alleyway to a secret neighborhood by the beach, and it's secret beauty and secret beauties. How ironic this secret monastery and this beautiful nun turned out to be.

See, I always tie my segways together!

In many ways, April's story was a sad one. She'd been a promising young lady, having graduated high school at the top of her class and then going on to college at a prestigious university (though not U.V.A.). However, she'd never graduated from that prestigious university, because during her second year there, after having gotten a 4.0 GPA for both semesters of her freshman year, April was introduced to cocaine. She quickly became addicted to the garbage, and with the addiction came the sad, destructive lifestyle that so many addicts deal with. Promiscuous sex, abusive relationships, loss off job (in April's case, failing out of school), and often, and as was the case for April, homelessness.

"My parents still hate my guts," she told me while sharing her story with me. "And let me tell you, there's no love lost from my end. But I give them props, because they're raising my kids, and they're doing a good job of it."

"And you have no idea who their dads are?" I said.

"Dude," she said. "I don't even remember having sex with anyone. When I'd binge, it was like, blackout every time."

April did tell me many stories of, potentially, Bigfoot Sasquatch, and she shared with me her disbelief when she'd been transferred to the monastery and told of the secret. She'd started out her studies at a monastery in New York City, where she was from, but after leaving the grounds to party on three separate occasions, she'd been transferred to the monastery in the middle of the woods in Virginia.

"How can I confirm any of this?" I asked as I was getting out of the van she'd driven to take me home. It was my assumption that it was one of the very vans I'd seen on election day two years prior.

"Well," she said. "You can't, really. I mean, I'm not allowed to show you one and all, but…" she trailed off, and I felt hope rise in my chest. "I can tell you where one is buried," she said. "And you can try to find the grave. As long as you promise not to dig it up."

"I promise!" I said, sounding like a kid whose parents just gave them permission to do something special- maybe open one of the gifts under the tree on Christmas Eve. April gave me directions to where, potentially, a Bigfoot Sasquatch was buried. She warned me that it was heavily guarded by centuries, for it was the grave of the 'aged one.' One of the tribe's elders.

"And you can record it, if you want, because no one will believe you," she said. "Let me tell you," she continued. "The sisters and I are excellent at guarding our secrets."

"You've been pretty open with me," I said.

"Just wait," April said, smiling her coy, inviting smile, and after giving me directions to the grave of the aged one, she drove off, bound for the monastery hidden deep in the Blue Ridge Mountains of Virginia.

It didn't take me long to go looking for the grave of the aged one. And though it would take me until the following spring, this past spring, as a matter of fact, as of this writing, I actually found it! I'll save you the details by telling you to simply go watch the video I made of the hunt. It's on our YouTube channel, 'Homesteading Off The Grid,' and it's titled "Flanked

On All Sides And Followed Throughout He Keeps Going And Finds The Grave Of Bigfoot Sasquatch." Many of the people who watched that video asked 'who' I was talking about when I kept referring to 'her' and 'she' when speaking of the woman who'd told me of the grave. Well, if you were one of those people, now you know.

It was April.

And why do I bring all this up now? Why do I include this story in a 'Christmas edition' of Bigfoot Sasquatch stories?

Because recently, as in last week, I stopped by the monastery to see April. I'd bought a Christmas card for her, and I wanted to see if she was well. I wanted to thank her for leading me, by way of her somewhat shitty directions that took six months to figure out, to the grave of Bigfoot Sasquatch. And admittedly, I wanted to question her further on these creatures and why it was that she and her sisters were given the charge of guarding the secret of their existence in our area.

But April was not there.

According to the old biddy who answered the main office's door when I knocked, April had never been there. It was as if the woman didn't even exist.

"You were there when I met her," I said, recognizing the old bitty. "You threatened to castrate me with a gardening hoe!"

"Oh, dear," the old lady said. "I would never do such a thing. Especially to such a sweet young man like you."

I couldn't believe it. This very woman had been a man hating bitch two years before. But now she was acting like a sweet little grandmother. I was being had. And I *knew* it.

"Where is she!" I demanded. "April!"

"There's no April here," a voice came from behind the old biddy. I looked up, and there she was.

April!

"*You're* April!" I said. "It's me. Kevin. Remember?"

"My name is May," she said, and she smiled, coyly, knowing I'd catch the play on words. You know, that whole months of the year thing? "And I've never laid eyes on you in my life."

"Seriously?" I said, my voice letting her know I wasn't buying it, but she continued playing her game.

"Oh, I'd remember you," she said, giving me a onceover from head to toe.

"Now, May," the old biddy who I'd nearly forgotten was there said. "You go back to your room and say three Hail Marys and four Our Fathers." The old biddy then turned and looked at me, embarrassment on her face, and said, "she's not been through the change yet. She still gets honry," and then she shut the door in my face.

I left, taking the Christmas card I'd taken for April with me. I scratched out April's name when I got home and wrote the name of my mail carrier on it and left it in the mailbox for *her*, along with a fifty dollar bill. The card had cost me six dollars and fifty cents so someone was getting it.

I have no plans on going back to the monastery. I can figure out what happened. The night April gave me a ride home, she'd merely had loose lips. She was excited to talk to me. She hadn't seen a man in God only knew how long, well, God and his nuns, and she was just excited to talk to anyone other than the old hags with whom she lived and who saw day in and day out. She'd done a good job at protecting most of the secrets, but I knew that she knew she should have never told me of the grave.

I don't begrudge April for what she did last week (as of this writing), acting like she didn't know me and all. I know she's had her own struggles, and she still does. And despite not getting any more answers to the questions so many of us have about these creatures that are not supposed to exist, like, why some of us can see them and others can't, etc. etc. I still do wish her the best.

And like it said in the card that she never got. The card I'm sure the mail lady didn't even read after taking the fifty dollar bill out of its center. I do wish her a very Merry Christmas.

As I do each and every one of you reading this.

And as I do him, her, it or they, wherever he, she, it or they may be hiding this holiday season.

Merry Christmas!!!

The End